This book belongs to:

. . . .

For Mum, Dad and Felicity (darling),
and for my wonderful Grandma.

First published in Great Britain in 2010 by Andersen Press Ltd.,
20 Vauxhall Bridge Road, London SW1V 2SA.
Published in Australia by Random House Australia Pty.,
Level 3, 100 Pacific Highway, North Sydney, NSW 2060.
Copyright © Kate Slater, 2010

Colour separated in Switzerland by Photolitho AG, Zürich.
Printed and bound in Singapore by Tien Wah Press.
Kate Slater works in mixed media collage.

10   9   8   7   6   5   4   3   2   1

British Library Cataloguing in Publication Data available.
ISBN 978 1 84939 008 8 (Hardback) ISBN 978 1 84939 075 0 (Paperback)
This book has been printed on acid-free paper

Magpie's Treasure

Kate Slater

ANDERSEN PRESS

On a faraway hill, in
a lonely tree, lived
Magnus Magpie.
He spent lazy days
slurping the slimiest
worms and chasing
pheasants, and in the
evenings he went
out thieving.

Yes, unfortunately,
Magnus was a bird with
an eye for burglary.

He stole only the brightest, shiniest, most dazzling things
and stashed them secretly in a hollow at the top of his tree.

He stole a dancing diva's shimmering shoe . . .

. . . and pinched a pinnacle from
the Taj Mahal.

He stole crystal
chandeliers . . .

. . . and couldn't resist
shiny sweets.

He even took Her Majesty's most magnificent, emerald egg cup . . .

. . . and went absolutely **wild** in the button factory.

But the thing Magnus
wanted most of all was the
moon. It glowed more brightly than all
the treasure in his hoard. So one night, he
took a deep breath and took off
towards the stars.

Magnus flew higher than
he had ever flown before, and just
as he thought he could not flap another feather,
not even for fifty fried worms, he reached the moon.

But the moon
wasn't shiny
at all!

It was dusty and grey and covered with rocks.

"Dull as woodlouse stew," cawed Magnus crossly, "stupid, mouldy old moon!"

He felt very tired and lonely.
He wanted to go home.

Magnus looked around for his tree, but all he could see was
the great big, star-speckled blackness. He began to cry.

Then, all of a sudden, his burglar's eye spotted something dazzling through the darkness like thousands of emeralds and sapphires.

"HOME!" he cried.

With a joyful cackle, Magnus
soared up into the air and flew
as fast as he could towards
the gleaming light.

Magnus forgot he was tired as he hurtled through space. Whizzing over the earth, he didn't even glance at the glittering landmarks below.

He made a beeline for his tree.

When Magnus finally reached home, he had quite a shock. There, in his tree, a glossy-winged magpie was enjoying a beetly breakfast.

"Care for a leg?" she asked, as she munched on a mouthful of maybug.

Magnus peered
into his nest.

His treasure seemed to have lost its sparkle.
Diamonds seemed a bit too flashy for a magpie.
He decided to give up burgling for good.

Magnus Magpie still spends his days slurping up worms and chasing pheasants, but he is no longer alone. And what happened to Magnus's treasure? He took it all back. Every single bit.

Well, except for
one thing . . .

. . . and he found a very
good use for that.

Other books to discover:

9781842709436

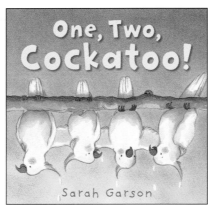

9781842709443

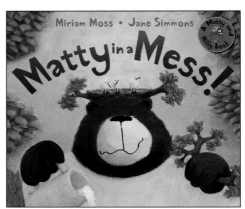

9781842709467

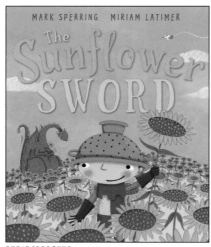

9781849390576

9781842709481

9781842709672